Where The River Meets The Sky

Jim Quartieri

ISBN: 0-9823546-0-6
ISBN-13: 9780982354605

Visit www.*booksurge*.com to order additional copies.

Dedication and credits

To Lama Kunga Rinpoche and Dr. Alain Youell, who guided me in the development of the heart, and showed me how to express the knowledge of compassionate wisdom.

With special acknowledgment to my son, John Quartieri and my friend, Janice Magrath, who together, assisted me in editing the final drafts with their distinctive and precise styles. John's inborn knowledge of writing was an invaluable contribution to this book.

Photography by John Quartieri.

To my love and respect for India, the natural environment and in particular, the river.

To the reader

'Where The River Meets The Sky' shows the relevance of the teacher-student relationship on the spiritual path. However, there is no way to completely explain the unique relationship between a genuine spiritual teacher and his or her student. What can be told is the story of one's own experience, and I have thoroughly incorporated many teachings here for the benefit of sharing them with others.

Being unable to write a word of prose for the first ten years of my writing life, it occurred to me to record my thoughts through my poetry in a prose form. The result is a Thoreau/Gibran style.

India's varied landscapes are mentioned in depth, with appropriately placed poems throughout, set in the time of the Buddha, 2500 years ago. Two ascetics travel throughout India teaching the art of meditation, living a spiritual life in the mundane world, and commitment to the goal of enlightenment. The experiences that the characters go through allow them to unfold their consciousness to real awareness.

Contents

Yesterday it shined upon me from a creativity that exceeds explanation. Galleries are full of replicas today. I find my life inside a gallery where replicated change evolves inside the finite creation of infiniteness. One, the number and the meaning have been repeated. Most often such simple truth is beyond our complications.

John Quartieri

Into The Flow Of All Things

The wind complements the energy flow of the river, as wands of light sift through and soften the bamboo grove.

Walking in the early morning the two ascetics saw the forest bursting with movement. Streams of light that pin-pricked through a flock of birds were brushed by the wind from tree to tree. Butterflies rested on leaves eager to soak up the first glimpses of sunshine.

After many years of separation, Vanadev met his closest friend, Ishwara, who was believed to have achieved the state of complete enlightenment. Like flames within a fire, the grasses became filled with warmth and lit with light. The two travelers took on a more peaceful gentle mood because of what they saw and shared together. In the thick of the forest they saw young ferns cloaked in the stillness of the mist. They heard the voice of the air and inhaled its morning scent. They felt the pulse of the wind's current as it brushed against them. In the embracing breeze, fragile blossoms within the wind blew on... Each day Ishwara and Vanadev walked in the forest, speaking little but paying attention to every sound. Sometimes, when night came they continued walking; the sounds of the forest and the light from the moon became their inviting guides.

As morning approached, Ishwara and Vanadev went into the forest to replace the poles and paddles for Ishwara's raft that had worn out from long use. Ishwara showed Vanadev how to select the proper trees to cut, they needed to be light but strong and flexible. He taught Vanadev the process of turning the bare bamboo into the usable tools they needed. After finishing they returned to the river and rested in the shade away from the Indian heat.

The sunshine withdrew its last rays from the land and they stopped to sleep where they had stood in the meadow. Within the darkness Ishwara passed a dream to Vanadev. 'From the seed of birth we were protected and nourished, the rivers of our eyes flowed into one another and as we projected our lives into the contemplative world of the monastery, we progressed in the understanding of compassion toward others. We were drawn into the ever moving stream of life's source and the longing for universal awareness gripped us. We sought the true nature of all things and understood the essence of the Buddha, which needed to be shared with all creatures. We opened ourselves to His breeze, stirring patterns in our hearts. And now that breeze will become silent and still, and soon the searching from millions of lifetimes will be fulfilled.'

Upon awakening, Vanadev remembered the dream and knew that Ishwara had sent it to him. They began walking in the direction of the river and soon Ishwara's body became a prism of iridescence. Coloration rebounded onto the ground and back to him. He radiated colors to the sky which shone like a rainbow and brilliantly lit the trees as if on fire. The meadows danced and sang as golden flowing hair.

"Vanadev, I am light, I do not reveal this perfected natural state to others because I must appear to be a simple man, so my work can be done unobstructed. Every person sees and reacts to me in a different way; every individual needs to be approached according to their level of experience. Some people respond to me as an ascetic, others see me as a nature mysticist, and to travelers I am the ferryboat driver. You are seeing the true nature of my being, it is the universal-body which is light itself. For too long you have tried to separate matter from spirit, but to advance on the path you must understand that they are inseparable. It is impossible to reach Buddhahood without this human form. Spirit and matter follow each other and permeate each other."

The distant blue mountains, ringed with mist, pointed above the blossoming dawn. The white sun began to reveal its presence, awakening the dew on the grasses into a meadow of reflection. The familiar river called them to sit by it and Ishwara spoke, "the fundamental rhythms in the world of form repeat: birth, heart beats, breathing, decay, death, and rebirth, just as one breath is exhaled, another is taken. But it is the light, the energy behind the cosmic river of illusion that continues, that lives on in the rhythm of life. A river is not simply water but the lifeblood of the earth, pulsing through the mountain's veins, directly to the ocean's heart which beats inside all of us."

Ishwara picked up a leaf and said, "this symbolizes a form within all forms, growing, changing, renewing. The river is all language, every language, speaking the same pure rhythm. The river carries the forms and the language through its deep waters into the sea. It is sacred and fertile, the source of simplicity and life, where all life becomes "one" when it returns."

Ishwara drew to himself quiet. A deep silence reflected in him. It seemed to Vanadev that the river had eased its flow as well. In silent awareness they sat gazing into the swell of whiteness and the surge of sound.

"Ishwara, if only I could be as consistent in my feelings as the river is with its patterned flow. If only I could form my ignorance into rocks and throw them far into the rapids to be transformed, then find myself purified by the reverberation of the white waters. Like a ray of sunlight I want to be forever held in the brightness, at "one" with all creatures. If only I could love you, my friend, as completely as you love me."

"Vanadev, you are sincere and much closer than you may think, you speak from within..."

For days Ishwara and Vanadev sat quietly by the powerful waters. Vanadev's understanding grew profoundly during this time. His goal of realizing perfection came nearer, but the time had not yet come for him to enter into the flow of all things.

Impermanence

Much time had passed and one season began to gaze through the prism of another. Sunshine barely brushed the ground, hesitating clouds gathered and reflected in stagnant meadow pools. The monsoon morning advanced, countless leaves gathered on the forest paths and painted summer with dashes of yellow and red. The meadow birds escaped to sheltered homes in the jungle. Deep blue, black, and red feathers sliced the sky, flowering into a collage of colorful shapes. Long shadows of naked branches touched the surface of deep reflecting ponds. Soon a white moon appeared and silence purified the air.

Another night, another morning, the cooler wind brought change with every breeze. Open to the silent motion, Vanadev and Ishwara watched falling leaves descend, without struggle onto the forest floor.

The almost empty trees whistled while each last surviving leaf became a chime caught between the light and the wind.

To prepare for the monsoon season Ishwara and Vanadev tightened the bamboo slats on their hut, added extra shoots for support, and placed another layer of reeds and grass on top. They built a fire and cooked fresh fish that they caught that morning and relaxed from the day's work. They ate and watched the fire glow, and then Vanadev asked a question that needed to be asked for a long time. "Did you not leave the Buddha and His teachings because you thought you could reach enlightenment without His instruction?"

"My dear friend, the teachings of the Buddha are priceless. They grace every heart that hears them and indeed everyone should have the opportunity to hear them. But I chose to follow my own path. Consequently I fell into much suffering that was unnecessary. If I had remained under the Buddha's guidance and protection He would have taken me through the passage of my karma while helping me to understand the ramifications of the difficulties that were to come. Instead, I chose to go my own way, but my own way was extremely difficult. When I made the choice I did not understand why I should stay with Him. He was Perfection Itself and He wanted me to stay, that should have been reason enough. You were correct to stay with the Buddha until His passing. Now it is necessary to remain with me, to share my life of harmonious humility." Vanadev got up and brought more wood for the fire. He was proud to share his time with Ishwara and live so simply.

As Vanadev placed the wood into the flames, Ishwara said, "fire is impermanent as is a human life. One flame, one second, seventy years of life, there is no difference, time is nonexistent. But whether one has a short or an extended lifetime they must use that space to understand the sameness of all life. As the fire becomes red and blue, it grows and takes refuge within the light. The heat, the colors and the mood deepen. Then the wandering energy moves upward into the infinity of the darkened sky; like a teacher's love for his disciple, never diminishing. Search Vanadev, search and let your heart feel the fire extending compassion into all the beings of the universe. Feel the fire burning within all of the realms of existence and discover your own nature."

A bit surprised and overwhelmed, Vanadev nodded in appreciation and agreement as the two ascetics bedded down for the night. Vanadev fell asleep thinking of the things Ishwara had said to him.

The next day rain dropped like a waterfall, everywhere at the same time without ceasing. Ishwara and Vanadev scrambled from their hut to make sure the cache of wood was still dry. The wind had battered the wood shelter but most of it remained dry enough to start a fire for their morning meal.

"Ishwara, I had a dream last night, I saw a man dying in the forest. He was too weak from a fall to make it back into town to get help. After several days of painful crawling, his swollen ankle had become infected. He knew that death was inevitable. He thought of his younger days and how easy it would have been for him to make a crutch and meander his way into town. He knew now that he was too weak from years spent battling the seasons in the forest to make it. He eventually died and I thought of how senseless it seemed for him to have lived through sickness and animal attacks, to survive all the struggles of his life in the wilderness, just to die alone."

"Vanadev, when a forest person leaves this physical existence, his form becomes nourishment for the insects, animals and birds. Even in death he has something valuable to offer. What remains will be touched by the sun, then eventually filter into the ground and become part of the soil. From this soil will sprout strands of wild grass for animals to graze on and flowers for bees to pollinate. Positive energy flows on, life to death and back to life, a circle that does not begin or end."

Vanadev looked into Ishwara's face and saw light, and through the light he saw Ishwara as a child, then a youth, their collective time spent with the Samanas in the forest. He saw both calm and suffering in the hearts of many who had known them both when they were students of Shakyamuni Buddha.

Vanadev saw all the illusory ages of man shining brightly, like all the stars in the universe, passing through Ishwara's form. His teacher held the knowledge of impermanence in all the realms of existence. Vanadev realized now that the Buddha and Ishwara were of the same infinite source and hoped that soon he too would realize his own true nature.

Ishwara and Vanadev meditated for what seemed an eternity, yet only a night had passed over the Ganges.

The Elusive Pearl

Deer among red leafed maples
ponder about in tall sweet blades of grass,
notes of song
lustily sung by two finches on twigs of bamboo.

The singers deftly sing their song
in flight, unaware of freedom,
only to grasp at air.
The deer eating too quickly to taste,
a noise - fear, they dash
to place distance, not knowing what from.

Bird and deer tire from guarding the unknown
they stumble upon the moonlit pond
drinking together, undisturbed
each sees their own reflection
though blinded to the symbolic light.

The finches peck at the reed,
the deer suckle the moon,
finally noticing the warmth -
duality subsides,
the new full moon
seeks other wanderers to serve.

The Profound Wisdom That Goes Beyond

Ishwara and Vanadev traveled from town to town, serving others selflessly in many different ways. In one village they came upon two men arguing. One of them, an artist, was painting the trees on the hillside, and the other was complaining because he felt the trees were perfect in themselves and thought that their image should not be imitated. Overhearing the conversation, Ishwara approached and said, "I was listening to you and may I offer this? A branch hanging over a pond is also represented in the reflection. Each is beautiful in their own way, and yet they are both the same picture in reality; as well as the person viewing them. So enjoy the trees, the painting and the painter, without discrimination." The two men looked at each other and laughed at their behavior. They asked Ishwara and Vanadev where they were from and where they were headed. The travelers answered politely and shared some of their food with the men. After eating they said their goodbyes and went on down the path.

While traveling through another town they passed by a prison where a prisoner caught sight of them and yelled, "you worthless wanderers, why don't you do something of value! Help me to escape from this unjust prison!"

Ishwara came up to the opening in the wall and remarked, "the Buddha said, 'that as a bee without harming the flower, its color or scent, flies away, collecting only the honey, even so should the sage wander in the village.'[1] So you see young man I have much to do in this village and I intend to help those who will accept my offerings and my service. Your request is quite the opposite of what I practice. I am not a worthless traveler because I travel with purpose. I am about to gather the honey from the hive, for the good of the entire village. I will find those whose lives will affect many others for a positive purpose and begin my ashram in the hills. When they are ready to share what they have learned I will ask some of them to go into the village to offer their wisdom and understanding. Furthermore, it is not so important that you seek help to escape from this building because the real prison is between your own ears. This you must conquer and escape from by yourself." The prisoner was silent but his eyes widened when he realized whom he was talking to, his father, Ishwara.

"Hello my son," continued Ishwara, "thirty years have not changed you much. You will know where to find me if you wish my friendship and my help."

As they walked away Vanadev asked, "I did not know you had a son. What is his name?" "It is Dakapouri. He ran away when he was twelve years old. He decided to live with his friends on the road instead of with me. He has had his share of empty pleasure, but he left me on his own and that is how he will have to return.

Ishwara and Vanadev began an ashram in a cave on a hillside. Like fallen leaves in a stream drawn down into the waterfall by the strong current, seekers were brought to Ishwara by the magnet of love.

One morning, after leading the meditation of the Heart Sutra which the Buddha had first given fifty years earlier, Ishwara asked his eight students if they had any comments or questions. One asked how karma and love are linked. Ishwara answered, "We must all shed our karmic impressions to find the peace within. We wind the impressions of our experiences around our subtle bodies, like a caterpillar makes a cocoon. We take them with us through lifetimes in worlds of matter as insects, fish, birds, animals, and finally humans.

"After millions of human lifetimes we eventually progress to the level where we commit to using unconditional love in every situation of life. This causes us to break out of our cocoon and fly toward reality, toward universal responsibility. Like a magnet, we draw impressions, many and varied, until we are experienced enough to repel them by extinguishing them through love. Until this release the magnet known as the law of karma will guide us.

"Much of a lifetime, whether coming into a situation or being released from one, we don't have very much to say in the matter, but progress is made depending on how we face the karma. The time of choice is now for those whose karma is interwoven with mine, and whose past life experiences have prepared them for a unique student teacher relationship; the time when mind and heart are motivated by unconditional love."

Two others, named Sudrulada and her husband Thrushami, asked Ishwara if they could remain in the ashram. "We would like to be free from the problems of village life. By leaving our home and residing here we could pray and learn your teachings every day."

Ishwara smiled, then paused and said, "being truly free is being happy wherever you are and helping others to realize this happiness. I do not want you to leave your home, and though I consider you both advanced in many ways, your karma must unfold there. To live in the world and understand and experience its complexities is a difficult challenge. You both have the awareness and the opportunity to spread unconditional love into society. People will come to you both some day for advice because the wise have much to give. This is your purpose!"

Ishwara closed his eyes for a moment then sat down at the face of the cave and lit incense that calmed the air. "Meditating or living in a cave is not necessary for spiritual advancement. If a teacher wants a student to live in seclusion then it is good for him or her to do so. It does not mean that the cave dwelling ascetic is more capable or more highly developed spiritually than the one who does not live in a cave.

"To meditate while sitting, a beginning aspirant naturally needs a quiet, pleasant surrounding in which he can concentrate better and be disturbed less, but a person does not need to be in seclusion to achieve this. Listen very carefully, too many sects complicate spiritual life. Some say that you cannot live a spiritual life without being in high places or in retreat. In general, a lack of the material world and lack of family life is embraced by many who seek the spiritual path. But how can the two types of life possibly be distinct when they are two currents of the same river? Everything is connected. You cannot reject one facet of life for another, if you do, you withdraw a segment of your experience."

Ishwara got up and waived his hand over the view of the trees and the valley and said, "The only reason for our existence is to learn how to love ourselves and others, and to allow ourselves to be loved in return. It is very important that you all understand these things because we are in a position to help those we come in contact with. We are all drawn together; our connection is the lifeblood from previous times spent together. Like priceless pearls strung with gold we are devoted to each other and to assisting all of mankind because of this connection. Like the lotus blossom, we can discover our interrelatedness with all beings, depending on how much we strive to cultivate that connection of love from within. This great responsibility is now yours to accept."

Silence followed Ishwara's words into the night.

Love Thrives On Itself

Although Vanadev had been one of the Buddha's many monks for several years, he thought it was the right time to ask Ishwara to become his new teacher. Ishwara only had a few younger students but Vanadev knew that numbers on the journey to enlightenment didn't matter, only the exalted state of the Master and his own propensity to perfect the art of loving.

"Ishwara, we were always friends and lifelong seekers of the truth, and I would be grateful to take on the role of your student; for you hold the perfection that I seek." As Vanadev said this, a tear came from Ishwara's eye. Vanadev was surprised, and wondered why he cried, but he acted as if not to notice.

Ishwara bowed down with great respect to the man who spoke from his heart. He understood that Vanadev wished to open his heart to his new teacher. Ishwara pictured this union as the symbolism of every drop of the river's water, every leaf on every tree and every ray of light coming together.

Vanadev took the bow and the tear as confirmation of the discipleship that he sought. He expressed his gratitude and overwhelming joy and fell into the arms of the one he so dearly loved, spiritually exhausted. Ishwara embraced his friend, in silence. For years he had wanted to extend these feelings to the Avatar, Shakyamuni Buddha, but they were contained in a heart not yet ripe for the deeper levels of spiritual expression.

The next morning found Ishwara holding a ceremony for his students called the empowerment of wisdom. Afterward, Ishwara asked three students to play a flute, a drum, and bells. Upon finishing several pieces he told them, "a musician or composer can be either male or female, but music cannot be either masculine or feminine. Music is always a combination of the two roles, they are inseparable. One string vibrates at a different frequency than the next, the most profound combinations of these being written with the composer tapping deeply into the notes of the spiritual heart. Music that leads the heart to sing will allow inner strength to grow. If you listen close enough to the physical heart you will find that it also has a rhythm, different tempos and frequencies, within it.

"Within certain pieces of music there can be heard, seen and felt, every type of song. Like the river, what one drop knows and feels, so ultimately will every drop, everywhere, at all times know and feel. From one song others arise, they link all other types of music to them.

"Music and voice are "one". When a person has experienced many lifetimes, and he learns to sing like the wind; like an instrument, his tone can tell of the quality of his experiences, his emotions, tendencies and the attributes in those lifetimes. By listening to the notes and words one can see the mountains he sings of and feel the sunshine. One can even begin to know the townspeople that he sings about. You would know their hardships and sense their skills and patience. This is what you will come to know about the music of life. Through the present moment you will allow the understanding of the past to come alive in you.

"A fellow ascetic I once knew had a likeable voice that was clear and calm. His tone was beautiful and whether speaking or singing it was inviting and pleasing. Expression is not merely words, but also the tone, the manner, and how much you understand yourself. Being expressive adds dimension to all you say. Communication means expressing yourself to others and receiving their expression in return. The feelings you project, more than the words themselves, are what the others will remember. They will be the basis for their impression of you when honesty and attitude walk the same path.

"There are many forms of expression and communication; singing, dancing, acting, speaking, the senses of touch and smell, one's vibrational level, the linking of the spirit, and so on. The expression of the heart is what directly touches the other person; this energy is what links all forms of expression together in communication. Correct posture and breathing is also very necessary. Rhythm eliminates compulsion. Slow and deep breathing removes tension from the entire body, the speech is consistently clear and this allows you to be completely understood by the other person."

The rains unexpectedly withdrew, and as Ishwara led the students down the mountain to the river, they passed through a low-lying meadow strung with the songs of singing birds, like beads on a string. Soft winds carried the suns rays and caused the wet meadow to come alive and glisten. Along the shoreline, the river carried thousands of wildflowers which fell to the water's sway.

The next day Vanadev broke up an argument between two of the students and asked Ishwara to speak with them. Ishwara said, "some of you at the ashram are always in conflict with each other. Well it should be remembered that you are sharing a very unique experience together as my students. Each of you brings something special to the group and it is foolish to overlook these qualities. If a problem arises, such as when there are complaints about one's appearance or temperament, talk it over, learn to communicate. Place into practice among yourselves what I mentioned earlier. Listening to the other person is the key. It is the other half-circle that completes the process of communication. Try to understand, wholeheartedly, what the other person is really saying, likewise your concern for them will grow and your conversations will become more constructive."

"Guru," one of the disciples said, "I am having a great deal of trouble with my work. It seems to become more difficult to perform the job each day. Should I simply quit and find another type of work?"

Ishwara answered, "if you left your job, you would only find the same situation arising in a different environment. You can quit a job, but not a process. Sometimes your work appears more difficult than it actually is because of the mental pressure you place upon yourself through worry, laziness, and negativity. When thinking about how difficult something is, you have the opportunity to apply a positive attitude and turn the event around. Whether you think you like the work or not, you must strive to enjoy it. Realize that any situation can teach you a great deal and that "practical" thinking ultimately makes everything easier and more enjoyable. When you realize that you are not enjoying a situation, tell yourself that you are and observe the changes that happen."

"But teacher, I am constantly sick and it makes my work impossible. What can I do?"

"Sickness helps to balance out karma whether you see it that way or not. Working creatively with this knowledge gives you courage, confidence, discipline, and an overall positive view of the situation."

"Guru, how can I change this then? You say creatively and with discipline, but I don't understand."

"It takes a little effort on your part, you see, you must allow yourself to accept a different outlook. When you are ill you must accept it and see the beauty that has been created for you."

"Guru, when I become ill, is it for my benefit? There is beauty in that? You speak of nonsense!"

Ishwara responded, "many people fear their illnesses, they worry about their obligations to their family and their work. They become frustrated because they cannot perform those duties. By keeping anger and frustration out of the way you can work through your karma more quickly. You will start to feel better when you accept your illness as a process of life, just as you accept taking a drink of water.

"If you do not accept your illness you will eventually become well but I am giving you the key to get through this more easily. Whether a horse is willing to pull a plow or is made to pull it, it is easier on him if he is dedicated to the task. If the horse works out of respect for his owner he would not only please him but get the job done sooner. In your case, and that of many others, your illness is being used for a purpose. It is like the river that overflows and fills a valley, uprooting many plants, yet makes the soil that much richer when it recedes. Illness becomes the friction that wears away the layers of your karmic knots. So you see there is beauty in this process!" The student bowed to the Master, out of respect.

Another person inquired, "Ishwara, I'm drawn to many women but I see the benefit of married life. However I can't seem to find a partner for marriage. Can you explain what I should do?"

Ishwara answered, "you can learn the deeper nature of people without committing yourself in marriage. Patience is key, the one you seek you have not met. However, marriage can benefit many people, but it should not be taken lightly. To prepare for a lifetime with another you can practice communication, friendship, give and receive love, and accept others for themselves with all the people you meet. That is where the process of experience begins. This I ask all of you to do whether seeking a lifetime partner or not."

A group of Krishnas suddenly passed a short distance from the cave and Ishwara called to an old friend, "Saranam, how is your father's health?"

After exchanges, the Krishnas continued on their journey. Ishwara explained to his students, "I met Saranam when I was on a hillside observing a tiger eating the prey he had caught earlier. After he finished, he walked toward a spring to drink. While he drank and slowly walked off to find a place to sleep, Saranam and I talked about many topics. After most of them she always seemed to mention her father and his poor health.

This was obviously weighing heavily on her emotions so I explained to her that she was cruel to him in another life and now had the opportunity to balance those impressions. I said that all she needed to do was care for him in a loving manner, simply by making him comfortable, thus learning how to best share his suffering.

"I told her that regardless of the past, whether you are balancing out something you have caused, or showing someone who was mean-spirited toward you how to be kind, each situation should be viewed from both sides. As in everything, love always brings equality to whatever you share.

"The analogy I gave her was: spring storms add water to the streams of melted snow, soon they join other streams racing down the mountain. The raging river collects sand, rocks, and plants and it never ceases to flow. Everything that falls into it is taken away and is smoothed by the tumbling of the rapids... so the appearance of it changes all the time. In the same way, love grows and thrives on itself and everyone it comes in contact with. It renews the faces and the hearts of all those it touches. Although experiences of love can be painful, it is the loss of love that is the cause of the pain. Without the realization of the necessity of these experiences, life cannot be fully understood. Love is the universal key to the lock of creation. Embrace it and share it for it is the only way to become the essence of all things."

Compassion Wisdom Skillful Means

Ishwara led the students into the wilderness. He taught them to walk quietly, but swiftly, and to stay alert like a mountain cat stepping over fallen branches. Ishwara's son, Dakapouri, had been patiently following and watching the group from a distance, while they practiced walking. He slowly made his way to the back of the group. They hiked along one mountainside and onto and over another until they came to a clearing.

The air was moist with dew and it carried the scent of the grass, brush, and earth. When they inhaled they could feel the chilled moisture bite at their noses. The practice of their newly learned walking was on their minds and no one wanted to be the first to break the quietude of their silent walking. They moved smoothly as in one motion, everyone working together. They noticed seeing more wildlife than before because the animals didn't feel the need to flee.

Dakapouri certainly didn't want to disrupt the group's silence but he had questions for his father that he held inside for many years. He marveled at the accomplishments that the silent walking achieved. He thought of how amazing it was that so many people could be welcomed in a meadow filled with so much life. He wondered if this tactic could be applied to other areas of his life. This interest sparked his mind and a smile glowed across his face because he realized that there was more than one reason for Ishwara showing them this special walk. He wished he could tell the group but he swallowed his excitement and instead thought of the many things he could now accomplish with patience and tactfulness.

He knew he could! He realized that this gave him a heightened sense of confidence, that he could debate and express his point in any situation simply by not arguing. He wondered if anyone else was thinking as he was. He pictured himself floating on the soft morning breeze: leaving his old ways and instead of pushing through life and grabbing at what he could, he would use these new teachings instead.

Transcendence

**Birds in a thicket of bamboo and plum
float on air, caterpillar on maple leaf
daydreaming of immortality.**

**The fragrant blossom knows
the last drop of nectar
the bee neglects is the sweetest.**

**True to its formless color
the rust painted sunset, my mind,
melts into the waiting sea,
non-existent, the expression of immortality.**

Soon they sat to rest and waited for Ishwara to speak. Dakapouri then came close and sat with the rest of the group.

"Father," Dakapouri said, "what is positive energy?"
"Ah my son, I am pleased that you have joined us. Positive energy is when the meditation becomes real. When a person is cheerful, under any circumstance, and always sees the positiveness in someone or a situation, instead of the negative, a productive chain reaction is created which sets up the next situation in a good light. Energy flows into you, as your wisdom and power grow, it radiates from you in all your thoughts, feelings, and actions.

"Positive thoughts are like a gust of wind propelling you into other positive thoughts and actions. Apparent failures aren't as significant and the emphasis is not on the actions themselves, rather the lesson's learned. We are here now in this space because we have put our energy into being who we are. What we do affects us immensely, good or not so good, it is our attitudes, intentions, and actions that make the difference."

Dakapouri then asked, "tell me about the aspects of love in connection with your group." Ishwara appeared almost joyous at the question. To him this was confirmation that his son was finally delving into the depths of his soul for the meaning to his life's unanswered questions.

Ishwara said, "like the sun in the desert which at one point or another will touch every single grain of sand, so too can love reach every single heart in the universe. Every grain of sand has its own set of impressions. Not one has had the same amount of sun, rain, or winds touch it exactly like the other. Yet they are all part of the same desert. As with human beings, each is different, yet each is of the same source of love. One's compassion for another binds this love to grow stronger.

"An ancient Indian story tells of a farmer who was standing in his field, desperate for rain, because his crops would soon die without it. Seeing the frustration and the helplessness within him, the sky, out of sensitivity and compassion, cried for him and his field. One drop followed another, in anticipation of his relief and happiness. Soon the sky swelled with tears and they poured over the land. The man fell to his knees in amazement and the crops grew out of the compassion from the sky.

"You are all drawn to me to perfect the art of love. I have accomplished what you seek to accomplish. In essence you are asking me to assist each of you on your journey toward realizing your infinite oneness with reality.

"But as in farming, first the land needs to be cleared. Obstacles, such as trees are removed, this is symbolic for the removal of negative thoughts in the mind. The correct attitude can be pictured as the seeds, which need to be planted at the proper time and in the proper manner in order for them to grow. Care and instruction water the garden of discipline and action, finally breeding confidence and ripening with the example of love from a Perfected One. The proper step at the right time is needed to ensure success."

As you develop and become stronger
you will soar like a bird to the next level of awareness,
like a hummingbird
with wings that seem to contradict time
with their swiftness
appear as still as the flower
as it surrenders its nectar.

"Through sitting meditation and meditation in action, this group will collectively send positive energy to mankind. As we perfect our awareness and understanding of the needs of others we will refine our level of compassion so that we can become infinitely helpful to all beings. Whatever comes back to us is the essence of what we have perfected and given out. We have the opportunity to spread our positive energy throughout the universe; with the proper groundwork set in place we can continue our work.

"So my students, everything returns. You have made the connection with me again. Our karma has brought us back to each other, uniting our energies for the benefit of all."

Ishwara stood up and opened his arms to catch the warmth from the sun and said, "we can all become purifiers, like incense purifies air. By understanding the energy of people, their sicknesses, fears, potential, and their stage of spiritual development, we can help to transform the energy around them with our clear and direct positive light. It will pass through them and ignite the spark of awareness where recognition is made.

"Each of us carries the masculine and feminine archetype, the joining of the two sides of reality. By helping to remove negative elements and create positive situations for others to fulfill their karma, they can observe their self-destructive patterns and be aware of how their lives and actions affect others. All this helps you, as much as those directly concerned, to become more compassionate toward each other."

The group returned to the ashram and Ishwara asked Dakapouri to go with Jawahar and Padmabandhu to a nearby lake to catch fish for them. Dakapouri abruptly stated, "I am your son! I should not have to stoop to the level of gatherers! Send another one of your followers instead!"

"Dakapouri, one who wants to get away from his troubles is not fulfilling his responsibility to himself or those connected with him. When one is placed in a situation he must follow it through with effort and honesty. This is the best way to progress on the spiritual path. If you become angry, your emotions will lead you to many paths that are based out of ignorance." Dakapouri became embarrassed, and realized that his father was right. Ishwara's wisdom cut through him and he knew that he had forgotten the previous lessons that the silent walking had taught him.

Dakapouri and the others climbed down the hillside and began looking around fallen trees where they might find grubs or larvae that they could use for bait. They also found minnows in a creek which they placed in a bladder made for holding water. Padmabandhu and Jawahar were very good fishermen because they had fished for their families all their lives. Within a few hours they caught enough to feed their small group so they wrapped everything up and began the trip back.

That night, after everyone had eaten, Ishwara and Vanadev gave praise to the fishing group for their success. Ishwara gave formal introduction to Dakapouri and he was welcomed with humble bows. Sudrulada asked for silence and later they all gave thanks to the fish who had given their lives for the nourishment of the group.

After several days of meditation and discussion a man approached Ishwara and his students. He had a radiant and peaceful face and his movements were extremely graceful. He was an abbot from a temple in the mountain called Arunachala, above the town Tiruvannamalai, in Southern India. After greetings, he told Ishwara of a dream which he often experienced.

"I dream that I'm in a city devoid of substance, merely forms and shapes filled with light. Carried by a rainbow I float down a path with outrageously beautiful flowers whose faces shine brilliantly like suns. I'm told by the sky that I am approaching the Temple of Love. Although there is no sense of movement, or of high or low, I feel that the sky is above and that I actually start on the path and progress upon it until I come to where the Temple is.

"After entering the space where the Temple rests I hear a voice that says "The Dawn." Then I answer, where do you come from? But I don't get an answer. I start to think did that come from my imagination or me? Then I ask, do I create you for my pleasure, my necessity, or simply to be loved? Are you here to remind me to awake? To see more clearly? The voice then answers me: 'The Dawn is light and shadow, as mind to body. The night is a symbol for the opposite pole within each person that must be seen, understood and recognized. The night is a staff by which one gains support to climb the karmic mountain and see reality more clearly. As the yellow-white dawn rises, understanding awakens within. All the processes associated with numberless thoughts and actions become fully experienced and infused with profound love.'

"Then I hear, 'you created yourself to be loved and to love all others, so know that everything has purposeful meaning. If your intention is to live with that purpose you must be compassionate toward all others. Then the warmth can penetrate, like the sun, to even the most ignored and crippled heart. As light, if you send positive loving energy throughout space, you can go anywhere, endlessly, but if you think that you are limited then you are held within that confinement.'

"Ishwara, this dream has taught me well. When I was young I saw the woods and streams as something beautiful, but so vast that they overwhelmed me. As I grew older I could see that they were part of my being. Now, they are a means that help me see through illusion; a necessary step in reaching the state of selflessness.

"In my understanding of the "night", I can see the other side of myself magnating toward separateness of identity and form. Not until I remove those forces can they be allowed to repel and scatter into nothingness.

"Motionless water reveals all I have experienced. I realize that love is undissipating, and is the nucleus of life, shrouded in shadows of illusion." Ishwara turned away from him, looked toward the ground, then nodded and raised his face to the sky and smiled. A moment later the sound of light rain could be heard, and as the clouds moved they could hear the rain coming closer. Ishwara turned to the abbot and said, "the Temple of Love is the final truth. You are the truth in everything and yet nothing; the fruition of all love and compassion. Your body of light is illumined in its true nature. At this moment the abbot died and became fully unconscious of the shadows of illusion. Countless Deities flashed across his now limitless mind and an indescribable white light blazed from every pore of his body to assist all the beings in the six realms toward their own enlightenment.

Between The Wind And The Sound

High in the Himalayas stood the magnificent monastery, called The White Gem. It was made of stone and was surrounded by gardens where tea and vegetables grew. Cascading steps led down to the shore of the Yamuna river where they bathed and fished.

Ishwara and Vanadev had been away for almost sixty years. It was home to them in their childhood; it was the basis for their spiritual development, where they learned all the not so simple lessons of growing up. Ishwara and Vanadev saw the need to return, they thought of why and how they had left, as two young monks who were eager to find the spiritual bliss sought by all they knew. Vanadev remembered his last conversation with his father, telling him that he needed to leave to follow his own path. His father had explained the difficulties involved with life outside the ashram but it was of no avail; he and Ishwara were determined. They were equally determined to follow their hearts' yearning and intuition, to discover their own way to realize God.

Ishwara gave instructions to his students concerning their daily activities and practices. He told the group that he and Vanadev would be leaving for a while to go to White Gem to share their spiritual discoveries from their time spent with the Samanas and the Buddha. He said that he was eager to hear the spiritual experiences of the abbot and monks from within a monastery setting. After a meal and short meditation the two set off on the path listening to the sounds of the wind through the forest canopy.

"Some at the monastery will not understand the reasons for us leaving our parents Vanadev. They will ask why we never returned to visit, even before our parents had passed. We will let them know that it was selfish of us to leave, and that once our eyes were closed but now they are opened. We had to discover our own way to find God within."

"Yes Ishwara, we will have many questions to answer and we may not be received well at first. We can only explain that when we were younger we followed our minds, and now we lead with our hearts, and our minds follow."

"Wisdom, Vanadev, is like the moon's light that finds the lake, and then sees its own reflection. It pleases me to think that we can return this gift to the ashram and explain that our separation from them was only but a reflection of youth, centered on immaturity of minds not yet calmed by the storm of silence." Vanadev nodded in agreement and struck his staff to the ground in acknowledgement of the truth and said, "I will show them what I have learned through humility of thought in action. I will bow to them in honor of my existence for them. I will wash away overindulgence in ritual and leave them with the manuscript of the Ganges to read. I will teach them how to pray to the vision of creation through complete silence and resurrection of the Boddhisattva within!

Ishwara and Vanadev kept on the path they named "quietude" for several more hours. The sun began to hide under the horizon and they picked a safe place to rest for the night in a fertile valley.

Night sounded the lights of the stars to awaken against the background of infinite space. "Ishwara, I can think of many things in life that inspire and that are appreciated but one moment spent gazing at the night sky reminds me of them all."

Ishwara added, "yes, when myriad light-beams enter our eyes, light that we could not see before this second illuminates our imaginations. Its journey from space took billions of years to reach earth and yet did not exist to us until we fixed our eyes on it. The bright dots set against the blue-black veil provide the perception of distance, time and the lack of time. They are all summoned into the forefront and backdrop of the mind and are seen as real. Nevertheless it is all illusion, nonexistent on the ultimate level."

Coyotes were heard in the distance making sounds of joy at a successful hunt. A few minutes of yelping and howling followed and the two men waited and hung on to the end of each sound the animals made, ever curious as to which sound was next. The dogs eventually returned quiet to the night and Ishwara pointed to the sky and expressed, "this immense beauty is to be enjoyed for what it is. I see it as a cosmic painting consisting of vapor, dust, gas, magnetism and solid matter combined with the action of explosion. It was painted by the Creator from reoccurring waves of imagination turned thought, then blazoned into expression." Ishwara rose and waived his arms across the sky, "infinite creative inspiration made the heavens and each speck of nature. The universe will continue to grow in its boundless darkness and light. Likewise, our own individual thoughts affect our own bodies and minds and we grow our thoughts in us and wear them like clothing."

Dawn awakes the land and dancing light rays warm the earth's skin with their rhythmic energy. Vines full with green leaves surge into life as the rays mingle with them and pervade their images. The stalks of the vines split the water of the creek causing it to go around them while countless vibrations leap into the sky and touch the light adding fuel to the multitudinous surges of energy. Each minute brings new warmth to the trees, rocks and dirt, causing metamorphosed energy to bound toward the sun and explode back into expression.

Ishwara and Vanadev continued down the path to the monastery. It seemed that wherever they looked, all was content and full of life. The wind sang songs through the reeds and the sound echoed in the ears of a hawk overhead. Ishwara's and Vanadev's connection to the land was spiritual, emotional and physical. Soon they came to the top of a hill and saw the White Gem aglow with the Himalayas as a backdrop. Bright orange sunshine rays arrowed into the earth. Flowers performed wildly as the wind caused them to dance in the spring heat. Their fragrant petals became saturated with sun currents as the streams of light exalted in the radiance.

After a few more hours of hiking they arrived at the base of the ashram. Before entering, Vanadev asked Ishwara, "can you tell me why it was important for me, and not another person, to incarnate here?"

Ishwara replied, "meeting in this lifetime was inevitable, we have much spiritual work to do together. Our connection at times has been painful, but this in fact helped bond our friendship; if everything was always perfect we wouldn't get the opportunity to prove our devotion to each other. Remember, we are together because the entire universe is affected by every one of its beings. With this in mind, we are here because, together, we can offer all beings our unique knowledge, wisdom, and love."

The Undissipating Drop Of Essence

The travelers were greeted warmly and with deep respect at the Hindu Temple. There were many students, some from as far away as Lanka and Japan. There wasn't a single person alive who knew Ishwara and Vanadev from their youth. Their ashes had been placed into the sweet Ganges and been reborn.

Many students were eager to hear stories from their travels. Seated at the river's edge, where Ishwara and Vanadev had bathed as children and later purified themselves as young monks, teachers and students listened while Ishwara described the nature of the spiritual journey.

"When the inner design of the personality takes form the vision for the aspirants' spiritual path is laid and the mind desires comprehension of knowledge. This growth must be wisely cultivated and fused with the understanding of the over-soul's intention. Suffering, or cause and effect, and the annihilation of the addiction to repeated patterns are the way of life. One begins to see their role in relation to mankind. Reasoning grounds and polarizes spirituality into balance. Each soul has a propensity toward spiritual progression whether or not the body-mind is conscious of this goal. Over time, karmic knots become more evident and the balance of tension or flexibility given to each knot is determined by the actions of one's experience.

"Both the spiritual, or inner, and the physical, or outer, workings of the individual are perceived to be separate but they must overlap to sustain this reality. Either one alone would dissolve the individual. It is important for each soul to be aware of their spiritual direction. Intuition steers the mind, the body takes direction, action and balance create equilibrium, this is the goal! If intuition and mind are separated the individual looses direction and the inner and outer workings become glazed and frozen, like trying to swim up a waterfall. Instead they overlap, and if the person cannot blend the two, his or her balance is disrupted and they can go no further. Spiritual progression is hampered until harmony is restored."

He paused to see whether they understood and then continued.

"As a person's spiritual awareness grows, their commitment to all beings becomes clearer. I call this pyramid-essence, and as like building a pyramid of stone, it takes one stone, then another and another, carefully and precisely placed in order. This is a slow process and patience must be taken. The life of the aspirant has many ups and downs, pitfalls abound, and the constant working, reworking and balancing is needed for the soul's path to remain clear. When the building blocks of love start to shape in this pyramid the soul looks upon itself and starts the process of refinement.

"One must look within and remove the rough edges of the stones of love before the next one can be placed, otherwise the foundation will not have the strength to withstand the elements of nature. After enough blocks have been raised, the heart and mind begin to compliment each other. With this enhanced wisdom the pyramid of the subtle, mental and physical bodies begin to work in unison.

"But even with this pyramid in place the seeker must remain dedicated to the teacher and to mediation. If steadfastly patient and superhumanly determined, the tendency to grasp for worldly desires becomes greatly diminished and the subject-object dichotomy can be put into perspective. When obstacles and difficulties are in sight we can begin to take steps to reduce their hardship. Surrender, devotion, and obedience to the guru will move him toward the correct view of reality.

"With much practice through meditation the mind and the body harmonize and become "one". An advanced spiritual teacher can help the student move through the levels of realization much more rapidly. Students who are ready may experience unrestrained energy, understand unlimited knowledge and feel an incomparable sense of calm. They may no longer see death as death, but life and no life as a rotating circle. With the pyramid completed, light emanates eternally. Attachment to finite sources has fully subsided. Imperceptible energy is flung into dynamic action and total compassion and wisdom are fed to every sentient being. Coming full-circle, the aspirant has completed the sleeping stage by awakening to the wisdom that goes beyond."

At the end of Ishwara's talk, the rays of the sun grew distinctly vibrant, and meditation followed until sunset.

When morning came the entire assembly of gurus and monks ascended the mountain with Ishwara and Vanadev. They sat in silence overlooking the monastery and the river, with the Himalayas to their backs in the distance. Vanadev was asked to tell them what the Buddha had taught him.

"The Buddha taught me that love is eternal, it is everywhere, and love is the one factor in everything.

He said, "it will be the love that mankind has shown toward itself that will lead us to the realization of the Truth!

"Once while walking into a serene autumn forest the Avatar told us that He was the breath of the universe; that He moved about in rainbow hues, crystallizing the mountains, the meadows, and the sea. He said He was the sun's rays returning to the source of all things, His infinity.

"Later I asked Him if I would ever come to know myself in this way, and He told me that what I seek is already a part of me, and all I had to do was clear away the extra pieces to reveal the Truth. Just as the spring leaf which already contains the deep colors of autumn within it, yet merely needs a climate change to release its colors, I had always been immersed in the quiet pond of infinitude.

"I was brought far along in my thinking by this analogy. I understood that I was the source that I needed to return to. The confused, worried, and impatient Vanadev was no more." Question followed anxious question, until the clouds curled into dusk and forced the mood of sunset to overtake the sky.

The next morning Vanadev told them how the Buddha assisted two married students of His. He explained that their responsibility to each other was to be honored by both of them. He talked of how important their dedication to each other's well being was. He polished their hearts and minds like rose crystals and said that they glowed like two stars in an empty sky. On one personal visit with Him the man sang a song of love to his wife which pleased the Buddha greatly.

"Later He sang it to me and now I will share it with you all.

"Touching your face I see your blossoming love, within your eyes I see our universe, an eternity together, your smile fills me with your essence, like a smooth breeze I float into your aura, my goddess of the sun...

"The song touched me deeply and reminded me of my own contemplations of marriage. The next day the Buddha, knowing my mind, said to me that some students need to live in the city while practicing because there is much work to be done there. To become completely balanced, more energy centered, some need to be grounded in the mundane every day routine samsaric situations. Some students who are with me now He said are being prepared for their next lifetime when they will enter this worldly existence. Yet for others under His direction, such as me, we can complete our practice in the forest. He finished by saying that each individual has a different purpose and unique path to enlightenment."

Ishwara led the assembly into meditation, "white water bursts off rocks and creates mist, rainbows arch the opening of the sky, everything is purified, calm, and the breeze is filled with fragrance. The original sound was OM, peace within itself. Then the primordial mind began to condition itself: separateness, unbearable sorrow, unthinkable loneliness and self-pity arose, leading to kalpas of desire, selfishness, and seas of anger. Concentrate on the world, after visualizing yourself already being One with the universe, surrounded by rings of Perfected Ones, each ring, larger than the next, extending through and beyond imagination. Look down from this high mountain to this dreamlike existence. Visualize your compassionate thought pervading ignorance, craving and suffering. Project this caring energy into every impression, thought, word and action.

"Extend intense penetrating light to all the beings in the six realms. Visualize the anger, frustration, boredom, disease, and humiliation completely dissipating, as all sentient beings empty their identity into the light of wisdom and compassion. Picture increased understanding and peacefulness rising in the hearts of every creature. See golden energy from God permeating all existence. Then watch the pain of isolation and innumerable fears become extinguished. Picture the karmic debts becoming balanced and the pain dissolving. Visualize an ant, a horse, a woman, a man, and every being, recognizing themselves as what they truly are. Rest for a long time with the light, the energy, and the OM mantra filling every heart."

Mirror Journey

After returning to the monastery, Ishwara and Vanadev toured the main meditation hall where they had spent countless hours chanting and listening to discourses when they were young. They visited the rooms where they had slept and played games. They hiked along ancient paths which they had discovered as children, and admired the majestic mountains that framed the lush forests.

Following a short retreat, the two Mahatmas were ready to leave the monastery for their return to the river. A few days later they said their farewells and several of the students gave them gifts of poetry, which were inspired by and written for them. They bowed and embraced each person warmly and left the monastery to read the poems in the forest.

While resting against moss covered boulders Ishwara explained to Vanadev, "while reading each poem, pronounce the words slowly and rhythmically. This creates an energy all of its own. I think it is important to read poetry out loud and also to yourself so you can observe the difference. The true meaning of the poetry can be understood in both ways but they affect the body differently. When you pronounce the words gracefully you are making the poem come alive within you. When reading to yourself, it is more of a mental understanding rather than a combination with the physical." Ishwara began to read the first of the priceless gifts offered in friendship and respect.

Mirror Journey

**The earth and I both from deep within
feel a oneness of breathing,
a vibration that warms, penetrates
overcomes the long sleep of endless lifetimes.
Prism scented air in the land of snow,
crystal streams awaken with the dawn
the bliss of a billion suns, purifies
transforms the mind into light.**

Moments of Consciousness

Vibration, from darkness to light
the seeds of morning take form,
leaves rest on the pond.

Fleeting clouds partially obstruct
weakened rays of sun essence
clinging to the remaining moments.

On the rim of the planet
the brushstroke into poetry,
bamboo leaves blowing in an autumn air.

The process of selflessness,
no grasping, no attachment
no compulsion to form a concept
equanimity.

The Teacher's Voice

Wind chiming through a crystal palace,
a stone falling through water,
the music within all motion.

A gentle and subtle ray of direct sunlight
fragrantly passing a flower
the silent essence of creativity.

Sunsets that wait at the end of the earth
suspended by sky and sea
held in the moment now, infinity.

The clanging bell united in motion
with the rhythmic passing of a vajra,
the unfathomable sound of mantras
vibrating throughout the universe.

The teacher's voice
emitting light to the six realms
as powerful and as impermanent as the sound.

Dao

Your tread is light
upon the path of the world,
deep roots, the eternal line
growing deeper and stronger
the tree of life from endless existences.
We draw the nourishment
to extend
the seeds rooted from the past,
the winds to blow
now and forever the inner energies.

Nectar

The abiding wind bending branches
the falling of crisp leaves through the air,
unfolding of truth in a single instant.
The ripples of water on the pond,
vibration of light from the Master.

Lotus blossom openness draws precise penetration
reflection from the water alive with energy.

The deep canyon between lofty mountain ranges
filled with the hollow form of silence
empty as the inner quiet of a cave.

Ishwara and Vanadev paused after reading each
poem to reflect on their meaning and also to think
about the monks who wrote them. They spoke of their
mental and spiritual growth over the recent time spent
together. After enjoying a cup of tea they read the
remainder of the writings.

While Resting at the Cliff's Edge

Wild wind spiraling through the sand
ripping billows from the sea
the meditation begins
lightning advances.

Distance fades to shadow to emptiness to snow
the unattached ocean intuitively surrenders
to the relentless frozen white sky
nowhere the observance of time.

The Sword and the String

Love and hate, concern and selfishness,
the energy which flows from one touches the other
attracts the other.
A sword has two sides
one to cut through spiritual materialism
one to gather negative attachments
to necessitate the cutting.
The same stroke creates both extremes.

Energy is like a tree
dispersion of the many branches.
Transmuting attitude and view to higher levels
causes one to pause at the sight of anger and ignorance
to reflect upon them until understanding appears.

A rigid mind is overactive
like a bow's string out of balance, inflexible.
Mistrust, illusion, and confusion swell
leading to misdirected destructive energy.
The mind's string if too loose becomes lax
needing to discover the space for perfect harmony
between discipline, serenity, and effort,
action, wisdom, and skillful means.

Of the Garden

Shaped by thousands of years of tradition,
ancient garden path
the clay of Japanese thought.

The cultivation of the heart
enhanced through the tea, the embroidery, the statue,
painting, the blossom, the refined focus.

Crossing the sea of karma,
stones placed between space
the method and the wisdom.

Nirvana and samsara
rooted firmly, growing as one
along the path of emptiness.

Continuity

The collective energy of all the Masters
gathers like brilliant white clouds
descending aura-like over the planet.
Powerful positive rays radiate toward every being
causing ego-mind to be revealed,
examined and transformed.

As the heart beats stronger
infusion of love purifies the chakra.
Immersion of wisdom, balance of compassion,
spontaneous action, collective energy
within the six realms is harmonized.
The cosmic heart is indestructible.

Gratitude

Freshness of dawn mist draws petals into opening
sun rhythms circulate as air, light, and flower merge
to realize oneness.
Sunlit winds spread the aura of light
into the depth of the universe.
Grasses bristle into solitude
whispering only for the wind.

Flute Song of Night

Smoke from the sunset fire rises,
perched birds upon reeds watch shadows disappear
serenely at the river with the OM sound.
Mesmerizing the landscape with solitude
holes etched in reed and bamboo are touched
like clouds covering a volcano
disguising energy eventually to be released.
One note following the other
the cause and effect of song.

Hypnotic magical path of the senses
takes final flight through the heart,
faces of a million starving, poverty-filled
enchanting Indian people
seen growing healthier, happier, more aware.
As they hear each note rising and lowering
they are transformed by the positive energy
wisdom, compassion, skillful means.

The Crystal View

With deep appreciation for the students who had written so gracefully, Ishwara and Vanadev sat in meditation in the opening of a cave high in the mountains. An eagle darted across their view of the brimming white sky. Its wings spread into the openness, circling and circling, as if drawing a mandala in the air. Light rays caught its deep black body as it soared down into the expanse of the emerald valley, far, far below. The warm energy of the sky rested on his smooth back, and his call awakened the morning of the forest. Through a cover of clouds, the eagle's image vanished, consumed by the sky.

"It is just like that Vanadev," instructed Ishwara, "that you will soon be open, free, unlimited, allowing yourself to be totally penetrated by my light and my instruction. You will carry the reality of the world in your heart and be consumed by your compassion, ready to enter into the flow of all things."

"Most Omniscient One," replied Vanadev, "you say that I am an advanced being, one with great potential and experience, yet I have no memory of my past lives, I have no knowledge of the other realms, or psychic occurrences, nor do I possess any of the secrets of the universe. So how can I be as you say?"

"Vanadev, the main areas in which you needed assistance was in the balancing of your attachment to karmic patterns of frustration, anger, self doubt, and lack of patience. In this lifetime you have allowed the Buddha, the Prince of Light, to share His heart essence with you and you have accepted my love as well.

"You have the ability to love unconditionally and as you apply it to each moment you grow closer to the ultimate realization. The Buddha, and now I, have kept your full awareness from you, as many teachers do with their students. It is the same when a person who as a master musician in his previous life can reincarnate and totally forget his previous knowledge and expertise of music. Yet he still has the depth and experience of it within him.

"Therefore, being unveiled and having the ability to feel the universe's energy and understand its workings would have distracted you from your current life's path. Before birth, your higher self decides which way is the most appropriate to fulfill your karma. Later on in life an advanced guide can determine if being unveiled is the most efficient method for helping you move forward in your growth. This unveiling must be used exclusively in an appropriate manner and with regard to the karmic consequences. In the past you have misused your power and damaged those in contact with you through jealousy, revenge, and anger. You were tempted to use your psychic power to prove to others that this made you more special than them. Your pride and incorrectly placed ambitions caused your spiritual progress to become subdued. To assure that this didn't happen again you were veiled from conscious knowledge of the subtle and mental worlds."

"Thank you Ishwara, this has answered many life long questions for me."

The teacher and his heart-disciple watched the valley lift its mid-morning veil as they stared into the golden heat, radiant, rhythmic, and strong. Ishwara stood and lifted his hiking staff, which he brought on all his walks. He called it his staff of light. It had served him for many years on treks over mountains, through valleys and across shallow parts of rivers and streams. They left the cave and went in the direction of the river. They came to a creek that leads to the river, drank and rested.

"Vanadev, to look into the mirror of a pond is to know the peace within silence. We should stay here and consume this silence." After a few hours the soft roundness of light landed its beam over the forest and the stars appeared like diamonds, glittering on the stage of the universe.

Days later the two sages met Sudrulada and Thrushami on the path. Sudrulada asked if they could return with them to the river, because their understanding of the connection between the spiritual life and marriage needed to be placed into perspective.

Unexpectedly, Ishwara began showing them how to do prostrations, telling them "prostrations in the most basic way make the body extremely strong. Muscles become firm and disciplined, the mood of the mind is calmed from the dedication of the humble process. The heart works harder and the body becomes awakened through its new rhythm.

"With humility generated, a positive attitude is attained. Bow before the Buddha, the Dharma, the Sangha, and the teacher. Imagine prostrating yourself in front of those, whom you dislike, visualize the differences between you and them disappearing. Picture the strength and awareness that others gain and at the same time, send light and love. Make every prostration a meditation for the benefit of others. Allow your body, mind and heart to become "one". As your pace increases, touch every heart with sincerity and try to forget yourself. Then expand your energy and let the compassion and wisdom within you flow out equally to the entire universe. Gradually you will become the compassion, the wisdom, and the universe."

They sat beneath a shade tree and Sudrulada said, "teacher, when I look into your eyes I picture a sun-overwhelmed garden with radiant clouds and bright flowers, I see gentleness of strength and a warm, soft energy. Your eyes are wise and clearly reflect the depth of your being, the tenderness in your heart left open to share your experience, your grace, and your compassion."

Ishwara warmly embraced her and said, "it takes an empty space for a crystal to form in the mountain, you have come with openness and without expectation, you have learned to unwind and let go. Soon all the conditions will be set for you to polish your heart like a crystal."

Ishwara then asked them what about their relationship needed further clarity. They asked him about the significance of sex and its connection in the spiritual life. He told them, "the energy between married people, or lovers, is the same as the energy of the stars. Stars have light, molecules, mass, and degrees of energy which are directly related to those within our bodies; the difference being that people are aware of their energy, of their connection and interdependence with all things. This energy can be directed toward all beings to assist them in completing their own universal responsibilities. Here is where sex, affection, and the deepest longing to join personalities come into play.

"In the art of love, sex ignites the energy within partners to respond in a positive way to love one another, awakening both of them to deeper levels in their relationship.

The energy level in the chakras will increase and greatly aid in eliminating sickness in your bodies, and allowing the subtle-body energies to flow through these channels, uninhibited.

A visualization during sex is to picture the world's partners giving of themselves to each other. During orgasm the energy flows and each person draws to his and her self all the creative forces in the universe, powerfully and equally. Each time you become less overwhelmed by the immense surge and are more capable of holding it, controlling it, and channeling the energy to all beings.

"Openness from both partners, through sharing and commitment, furthers the depth of their involvement. Energy flows through everyone, but to understand its existence and how it works with mindfulness, each individual must tap into and use it to gain higher awareness toward the understanding of real love."

Sudrulada and Thrushami looked at each other in loving acknowledgement.

"When you combine the visualization of golden light and the completeness of total love and gentleness toward your lover, you allow your feelings to become universal. With patience and practice, this will become easier. As soon as the essence of the sexual act is part of who you are as a couple, then the deeper rhythm and harmony in your relationship will energetically radiate toward others.

"Having sex lovingly shows that you appreciate each other even if you don't always make it evident in your daily lives. Love is the joining of separateness and ego with the initial stages of selflessness. But even sex in the art of love between couples creates attachment. This fire of love you feel for each other is but the beginning of real love. The completion stage of real love is the unawareness of "self". To eliminate individuality, instead of physically acting out your feelings of love toward your partner, you must come to the point where you allow yourselves to be consumed by this love; thus eliminating the physical desire.

"You see if you both were not "we", but "one", you would not see the need for sex. Do not try to rush this, you can be wonderful spiritual beings without pushing this. When the time for this transition is right it will happen without any effort on your part.

"The art of love is ancient between you and when you grasp the significance of real love, all your former life encounters and all of your present feelings, impressions and desires will be brought to each moment of awareness. They will disappear into oneness because the intention and the practice of love, harmony, and balance disintegrate its opposites."

Suddenly, the glare of day seemed to diminish as their clarity of understanding increased. As if the natural world were listening too, the fragrance of mountain flowers permeated the afternoon air.

Ishwara continued, "everything has its nucleus within everything else. Because of the inclination to assist all beings, when we are filled with the light of compassion and know how to release it, the light rebounds to us and increases our own ability to generate even more light. The power of the universe is within you. You will gain strength from each other and your commitment."

Thrushami replied, "Ishwara, this sounds wonderful and we would be honored to get to this level, but how can we wear away the friction each of us sometimes feel from living together, so that we can move toward smoother harmony as a couple?"

Ishwara answered, "in the state between physical death and rebirth, we are carried by the amount of energy we have generated in all our previous existences. This energy propels us where we can refine our experiences. I will give you a meditation for helping you both to be more understanding of each other. Sit facing one another, or visualize doing so, and try to see why, at times, you upset each other. See what has caused the problem and picture the solution by sending white light to each others hearts. Concentrate on the light and see the qualities that you appreciate in each other. Soon the trivial problems will dissipate and the deeper ones will become clearer and have less of a hold on you."

"Carry this into all you do together and you will have more insight to deal with situations as they arise. This positive exertion creates a responsible atmosphere which is one of the most direct ways to balance your karma together.

"Another meditation, which is also a valuable technique to use with friends or people whom you don't always get along with, is to place yourself in their position, feel how they feel, and through their eyes look back at yourself. This is real communication. Understand the feelings of others and show concern, whether you agree with them or not. Do not find fault. Finally, picture the entire world within you, with no imperfections and see the limitlessness within each of you. Know that whatever you do, you do out of love and respect. Admire this expression within you and let it grow.

"Unless you understand your deepest feelings for each other, and touch that part in your hearts where the other resides, how can true intimacy ever enter your relationship? All of your qualities of tenderness, respect, and kindness, which you consistently show each other, will move you toward the smoother harmony as a couple that you long for. Now go and find a secluded place and rest with these thoughts by simply sitting in silent embrace and allowing your hearts to perform."

Where The River Meets The Sky

A few days after the students left, Ishwara and Vanadev reached the river. It was mighty and green, and at places, placid and rainbow hued. The intrepid forest dwellers walked along the sandy beach to the cove where the ferryboat was tied and waved to those in boats floating by.

The next day they were taking passengers across the river and one of them from nearby Varanasi asked why the old men would bother to do this work.

Ishwara replied, "this is an auspicious place, there is much we all can learn from the river. Work, like anything else is a meditation, a meditation in action. A process is created and fulfilled and one process is tied to all processes, like the microcosm and macrocosm. When something is completed in the proper way, with the correct attitude, its relation to all facets of life can be seen. Because of life's chain reaction one can see the finality of a lesson learned and the beginning of another.

"Thinking constructively makes room for the pieces of the puzzle, and effort and wisdom allow them to fit into the situation. Regardless of what you do, the energy within you and the action are not separate. If you are a carpenter, shapes and measurements are used. When you lift something, balance and movement is involved, as in dancing. If one is a painter, colors and form are important, as in design."

The passenger interrupted, "but how can dancing and painting be the same?" Ishwara continued, "they are both undercurrents of the same river. When dancing, a person does not take erratic steps, but smooth properly spaced ones. The same with painting, predetermined even strokes are well placed. A person has the same attitude when walking; each breath is a controlled coming and going of their being. The method is oneness with the body and the environment.

"The attitude of a painter is also creative and useful. Body, breath, and mind harmonize to affect all the parts of one's form. In this union the spiritual side is embedded into the canvas. The method and wisdom are the same in walking or in painting, as with anything. The precise attitude and energy can be used and centered, and this leads to spontaneous dynamic action."

Another scoffed at Ishwara, saying, "and how should I view the washing of my clothes, as a purification rite?" "It is as important as you make it. Think of your chores as not being your work but the work of the Buddha. The thoughts that are in your mind while performing your duties, such as washing clothes, have an impact not only on your attitude but those who you interact with.

"Like a meditation, the clothes could be viewed as symbolic of the world's apparent faults, failures, and ignorance being dissolved. Placing the clothing to dry in the sun and air is also purification, the circle of change and, cause and effect. Creating positive situations is what creates perfect harmony. So you see, nothing needs to be boring or tedious when perceived in a certain way. Use creativity and imagination and you will be much happier."

Another passenger complained about his mundane routine and saw no connection with spirituality and his house cleaning job. Vanadev then added, "you should try to picture the health of the person whose house you are cleaning. Cleaning helps to eliminate negative feelings acquired or released by the occupants, which in turn helps to keep them from becoming ill. Organizing their environment helps them to see things more clearly as they go about their daily routines. People can function better in an orderly setting, they become less confused and more relaxed this way.

"Whether washing dishes, clothing or floors the spiritual process that takes place is up to you. With one-pointedness of mind the end result is purification. Each step within the process can be a meditation which is selflessly directed toward the person for whom you are cleaning. A positive attitude creates a pleasant environment.

"Meditation techniques should be incorporated into every aspect of any job. Take a flower arrangement, the essence in every action and every moment is the harmony and the cycle of beauty."

As the ferryboat reached the shore the people thanked Ishwara and Vanadev and wished them well.

Impressed with Vanadev, the young person who asked about house cleaning, who later would become Vanadev's student, stayed by the river and asked him how a person could determine if they were progressing along the spiritual path. Vanadev answered, "suppose a person finds a rough crystal deep within the mountains and works each day to smooth and polish it. Well, after some time the crystal will take on the energy of that person's personality and it will saturate his depth of love given to it. The quality of impressions he guided into the crystal, the energy of his will to do a complete and perfected act, and each stroke he used, are soaked in like summer rain to soft earth. What is placed in, is given off. What is imagined and projected, and skillfully imbedded, is what is reflected.

"In this vein I can add that like the crystal, every part of one's personality which needs refinement must undergo this same process. Positive rhythm eliminates compulsion. Whether in walking, chanting, talking, or with hand strokes while cleaning a shrine room floor, if smooth, even, and positive actions are used, a person moves forward in their growth."

"But sir, my mind is usually in a state of confusion! How can I create positive rhythm?"

"Within the concentration of each single stroke, or thought, is the present, the moment, now. This crushes the illusion of past and future and allows one to recognize the falsehood of death. There is never an end, only the "sense of now" in each situation that arises on its own, yet in conjunction with all things. Within every action or thought is the essence of the "now.""

The Impermanent Pond

The brushstroke is held firm
patiently waiting in the moment, now.
The reed tip touches mind
boundaries drawn, contemplation,
the origin of all existence.

Images, shadow, and space
dart between sunlight reflections
from pond to painter,
delicate gradations of ink tone.

**No separate manifestations
one continual thought of phenomena,
bird, rock, water, reed
reflects to sunlight to painter to breeze
ultimately no painter, no object, nothing to perceive.**

"Life must be accompanied by a sense of playfulness. When a person feels that they must go on because they have to stay alive, just to survive, and don't know what else they can do, then you know that this person has lost their playfulness, the sense of non-attachment. This seriousness leads to incorrect thinking, wrong views, and depression. One tends to see life as a duty, instead of the clear, diversified, and precious jewel that it is.

"Playfulness leads to creativity and joy, spontaneous love for whatever you are doing. This helps to lead to a greater kind of transformation of the menial and mundane tasks into something purposeful. Positive action increases our own understanding of the authenticity of things.

"To be playful minded and positive, and to transform a dull or even a horrifying experience into a helpful situation, or at least one that you can bear, is beginning to unravel the enigma of the moment, "now." When I say this, I don't mean that the past and future are not involved, or are not real to the moment, even though in ultimate reality none of them exist.

"What I mean is, suppose a farmer planted a seed which would not show through the surface until another season. The actual planting is in the present moment, and the existence of the seed and the occurrences that led up to the man becoming interested in farming are in the past. The resultant action from that planting of the seed would be the expectation which arises in the mind that it will in fact grow, when it will first appear, and what the crop will look like: that is to say, imagining that all this will actually happen.

"So while all three times are involved in that moment of "now", they are real in that sense, but the action that is of importance is the one in the present. When the present is perfect, the past and future blend harmoniously. The focus which the moment "now" brings to anything in life determines its value, understands its value, and respects and increases that value."

The young man replied, "but if I see an old woman in the present, I will see wrinkles and not youth."

Vanadev answered quickly, "there is nothing wrong with wrinkles. The energy of experience and spiritual wisdom that one has acquired is reflected in the eyes. When you understand the present moment you will see youth in everything and everyone. Age is an illusion. A kind heart never ages. When you place this wisdom into perspective and practice, you will understand its meaning. The fullness of being, is being who you are."

In a shy manner he asked, "Vanadev, is being who I am, enough?" "Be free and joyful like an arrow soaring, with concentration and one-pointedness of mind. Release your fears and indecision, and like a bow's string, keep your heart open and flexible. You are the motivator of your own freedom.

"The sunlight can change exquisite glass from one color to another in a single moment, so too can your attitude change your entire outlook and views of your personal universe. There will come a time, when you will be ready to enter into the flow of all things as if spotlighted by a shaft of sunlight. Your non-attachment, knowledge, karmic balance, and your infinite disciplined compassion will all come together and your mind will burst into light. All of your experiences and the means to their positive use will harmonize. You will completely understand that even if you possessed caves filled with gold and gems, boats brimming with rare incenses from all over the world, warehouses packed with beautiful brocades and paintings, you would have an infinite number of riches far greater than any of these.

"You will possess the freedom from countless self-bondages and know that you have mastered every conceivable lesson from life. Through oneness with all things you will understand the hearts of all beings, and serve each and every one toward the opening of their hearts to themselves. This is where the journey of spiritual life becomes completely selfless, where we return to the Source, to God, where the river meets the sky."

Ultimately Facing One's Reflection

After a week of work on the ferryboat, Ishwara and Vanadev sat outside Ishwara's old river shelter and watched the potency of the summer sun disappear. Golden-red clouds, stretched gracefully across the sky like the strands of a waterfall through the air.

In the warm night's quiet, the moon rose over the openness of the river and its light melted over the water. Free to wander through the meadow of space, the moon lured the attention of the two men as its light embraced them in softness.

"Ishwara, I finally understand the love you share with the river; the wind keeps pace with the flow, the reeds sway as they nestle next to it, the lapping of the tide on the bank echoes vibration, nurtured by the warm light kissing the curl of the current. The light and the wind and the sound give the feeling of the infinity of the sea..."

The two ascetics watched the moonlit water, deep into the night, until the sky awoke with the orange light of morning releasing its energy into all things. They bathed in the pure river waters and listened to the birds sing as they soared with the distance of motion that knows no time. They heard the hiss of the bamboo and fir trees stirring in soft sun ray winds.

With their backs to the river, they sat on the sand bank and took notice of the yellow-white snow on the shoulders of the remote mountains. Vanadev told Ishwara, "within every moment, distinct mountain features expand with the sunrise, the nearly invisible moon captures an eagle's passing, clouds magically appear in the sky, and blossoms take to the wind. The ecstasy of momentary discovery carries continuity and profusion.

"I see my lotus-mind opening more each day. Creativity, subtle clarity, and an immutable peace are all a patterned flow of interrelation with all the molecules of the universe." Then he prophetically stated, "in time, every living leaf holding to its source for guidance will become weak enough, therefore strong enough, to become totally unattached, and fall away.

"Ishwara, in my dream last night, I was watching the colorful leaves of a reflected tree and my ears were summoned by the wind carrying a flute song deep within the forest. The melody caught my heart and as I approached with a flower to bring to the flutist, the petals burst into countless deities, and I awoke."

Very lovingly and in a soft voice, Ishwara explained that he was the flute player calling to his friend, who was soon ready to enter into the flow of all things.

Ishwara asked Vanadev to bring him a flower. A few steps away grew a lone dandelion blossom, fragile and sublime. Vanadev bowed and laid it into the hands of the one he so dearly loved. At this moment his consciousness expanded into infinity...

For an instant there was total silence everywhere in the universe. Spirals of white clouds danced in the sun petrified rays, the trees weaved, and the wind twirled and flowed into rippling fields of grass. Softness lit every breeze as the sun bowed to all the flowers. Vanadev showered his body in the radiance of the sky and at that moment he knew that it was not important to know... God Realization overtook him like millions of cherry blossoms rushed into flight by the wind. He could feel every drop of the river answer to him in a patterned flow. Birds and animals gathered to gaze at the magnificent sight of imagination, fully expressed. Towering mountains smothered in white held both ends of a rainbow suspended above them, creating a prism in the valley for the one who had accomplished the nearly impossible.

Vanadev had entered the realm where only love reigns supreme. His enlightenment meant that he would no longer be subjected to the rounds of birth and death. Although he had become One with Reality and synonymous with God, he would retain the thoughts and impressions that made him an individual until the dropping of his body.

Silence thrived in glimpses of space as the celebration of solitude soon came to an end, and Vanadev waved the birds and animals back to their routines. He and Ishwara stood near the river and watched the rain begin to fall lightly. The ground tingled with moisture and light, dormant seeds awakened in the warmth.

That evening as the water glistened and the moonlight knelt low, the sky absorbed the feeling of oneness, cast by the two shadows below.

Closest to the OM Point

India, India
the passionate lover that inspires my soul
countless landscapes of impeccable beauty,
tradition, culture, variety, ancientness,
the search for wisdom
the path to enlightenment.

Flamboyant palaces and temples
a universe carved in stone,
sacrifice, surrender, commitment
born from the splendor of ardent devotion.

As the sun lowers itself below the mountain
I stand at the river of time
and watch my respect for India
blend into the sunset colors
until they merge and we become one.

The next day Ishwara left the shelter and went to gather his students. He returned a week later and sat with them on the shore of the Ganges. He said to them, "this group has committed itself to each other, and that means you should function with the positive qualities each of you have, to help others. Together you can generate the energy needed to love all beings and you can fulfill this commitment by visualizing our collective energy in situations of life which you find yourselves.

"You need to project your limitless positive energy toward all people through your everyday activities, even during sleep. You must envision a personality transformation culminating in the dissolution of a person's limitations and habitual patterns, and the ripening of their happiness and subsequent reaction of that happiness onto others.

"There are too many people wandering aimlessly in their own suffering. This ashram was formed from our karmic connections with each other, for our growth, and for the growth of others. All ashrams fashioned in this way, always, always make the most loving and lasting impressions on mankind. To increase the love within you and extend that love to others is precisely the beginning and the end of all personal and collective journeys.

"Courage, accompanied through caring and wisdom, form an indestructible personality that never stops seeking the truth regardless of obstacles or fears. All beings should be viewed with love and respect. If you present these aspects of compassion how can anyone be afraid to face any situation? Loving-kindness, and humility, with sincere purpose eliminates fear!

"If we admired the beauty of a certain flower, we wouldn't hesitate to enjoy its fragrance or touch its softness. In the same way, with equanimity you must expand your view of service to others, without reservation. It isn't enough to feel and accept love when we come together as a group, we need to fuse it into every aspect of our lives, therefore nourishing the lives of others.

"A meditation which will help to define and expand your unity and project it to others, is to first picture each of your bodies purified with intense white light. Then pass the light through each of your hearts. Watch as your hearts become so selflessly involved in all the conditions of humanity that they expand to include all the creatures in existence.

"The time for understanding your commitment is now, so allow it to happen. Move quickly and follow your hearts, keep in mind that ultimately, you are on this earth to serve."

While the students rested in the warm glow of this new knowledge, Ishwara asked if they were holding onto any unanswered questions. One of the students asked him, "what is the real essence of karma?"

"Along with what I have already told all of you, it is like a plant, something which seems to appear all at once, yet has taken a considerable amount of time to grow. Karma is something to be worked on with all-out effort, distinction given to the situation, the cause of it, and the remedy for it.

"The positive energy generated transmits to those persons or situations whom you have encountered in past life connections. Karma also is your chance to allow the effort of dynamic action to enter all you do. Dynamic action is a patient wisdom that transcends all doubt, and places thoughts and intentions into perspective with direction.

"It can be likened to acquiring a body which until now merely possessed the consciousness for one. After a bridge is built, it is the use of it which creates action.

Where there is hesitation, there is doubt, dynamic action "forgets" this doubt and acts from a spontaneous source of selfless intention."

Another student then spoke, "I am troubled by all these so-called advances and achievements in the cities today concerning inventions, and new methods for doing the things which we have done for many years."

Vanadev answered her, "the creativity placed in thinking of something in a different way, and the effort to see it become functional so that it can be useful for everyone, is positive growth. If an idea is better why shouldn't we be willing to change old patterns with which we've become attached?

"In times to come many changes will take place, but regardless of all that will come to be, there will still be suffering. Inventions will not make people any happier. In fact, people will have to learn how to become free of the attachment from their eventual dependence on these things. But then that's all part of the game of illusion. Things do not hold attachment, desire, or stupidity within themselves.

"That is one reason why we are here, to help us understand these things. So don't become discouraged, new ways are the natural course of things; a river never looks the same one moment to the next."

Vanadev went on, "any search in life is just the discovery of that which is already in existence, likewise in action-meditation, as a person looks for causes for her sufferings, she uncovers the remedies. The student eventually recognizes the fact that she is God, that the light she seeks is already within her."

Vanadev then reached behind where he was sitting and brought out a small box with several beautiful leaves inside.

"I have been collecting these leaves for a long time. They are from different valleys in this part of the country." He showed them the leaves and continued, "these leaves have energy-auras and can teach many things. In this leaf I see countless veins branching out for expression." Reaching for another leaf he explained, "this one reminds me of the grace, form, and the energy impressions of the other leaves and yet all have different root systems. I love these leaves. Everything is the Buddha-nature.

"Leaves have an affinity for the sun and wind and in a very subtle sense, know that they are destined to separate from the tree one day. Perhaps the tree communicates in its own way with its leaves, as I do with you. It is my responsibility, like the tree to its leaves, to assist Ishwara in helping you to discover your true nature.

"Concentration and attentiveness are energy. If you live every second in awareness of the truth you are living your life through meditation-in-action. The external world does not enter you, everything issues from you. Each of you is the source of the universe.

"One thing follows another, everything is interrelated. One intention, one thought, one action, is based on another. As light is issued from your hearts toward a person, everyone and everything is affected. It all begins with you and within you.

"When you come to know and eventually love someone, it is as though it just happened in that moment. Well, what is a moment? The truth is you have always loved that person, you have always loved everyone.

What occurs is merely a chain result from feelings and actions that you had set in motion in other lifetimes. One never needs to discover love, only to rediscover love. We are all images of the mirror of reflection. We are the essence of the Buddha-nature."

Heart Is Mind

The next day brought them to sit in the nearby meadow of bamboo and fir trees. Dakapouri asked about a poem written centuries ago, called 'Here Disguised in Meadow Breezes.' He said the author was unknown and wanted to know what it meant and who Ishwara thought might have written it. He read it aloud.

> **"The vanished lover here disguised in meadow breezes**
> **long awaited for in the vibrant brooks stirring,**
> **listen, she calls again, a birdsong, soft,**
> **tender, as morning drops of night on the leaves**
> **carrying the last specks of darkness into the light.**
>
> **"Listen, I hear her calling in the meadow silence**
> **come, come my lover, reach beyond time**
> **embrace the spirit of all things**
> **within you, blend the light and the darkness**
> **on and on forever, within you, touch me**
> **dance with me among fertile fields of flowers**
> **come, dance with me until the sun explodes our forms**
> **lifting us through the whiteness of the sky**
> **to unite forever within its endless clutch of beauty."**

Ishwara answered him, "the vanished lover is your heart, anyone's heart that has not reached Realization. It is waiting for the moment of union with the Divine Beloved. She, "your heart", is calling out to you, to come and embrace the spirit of all things; calling you to blend the imbalances and unite the opposite forces within you.

"It was told in a dream to a seeker by a Dakini. You are very fortunate to be concerned about this poem's meaning. Try now to fulfill it."

Ishwara asked those assembled if any other writings inspired them, and if they had any questions or comments about them.

Parvati said that the poem 'Oh My Beloved' was very special to her, and she read it aloud.

"My beloved, your calmness
likened only to the leaves without wind,
your beauty
likened only to the fullest extent
of earth rich with blossom,
your serenity
likened only to the sunset sky.

"I could sing a thousand words of you
and only a moment would pass,
a spontaneous moment, devoid of time and place
likened only to the leaves without wind
to the sunset sky
to the blossom
without which its fragrance is never lost."

She knew that the hidden meaning was a student talking to her teacher of her love for him. Ishwara agreed, and Vanadev poetically added, "the flaming rainbow arches the sky, the ancient depth of mystery fills the heavens. An eagle flies through the rainbow, the colors blend him purple and green and blue. He glides even higher to grasp the universe, the infant smiles not knowing why.

"You see, the spiritual infant, the student, sees beauty and perfection and admires it on a certain level. But not fully understanding it, not one with it yet, she longs to be near this perfection, and this is the teacher. This longing, is a rare and exquisite love."

Another student remarked, "I recently had the opportunity to share another ingredient of love's touch. One day my young son asked me what love was and I showed him the forest. We walked along a small brook and listened to it talk, ripple after ripple. We heard the music of the wind. I showed him a nest of newborn birds and they chirped at his wide-opened eyes. Soft penetrating light squeezed through the trees, a few leaves fell. We watched the sun grow dim from high up on the mountain, I hugged him, and he understood."

"That is beautiful," Vanadev replied, "that sense of selfless understanding goes far beyond intellect and in the advanced stage it surpasses feelings.

"In completion, in letting go, it is compassion which seals the endeavor, the relationship, or the situation with perfection. It finalizes the process in a positive atmosphere."

A student remarked that it was simply too difficult to see a certain person in a compassionate way. Ishwara answered, "you need to apply different methods and find the ones that work for you. You must be perceptive and creative in doing this, and that will lead to confidence. The other person will know that you are sincere and if all seems to fail, at least try to be friendly toward him or her and know that you have done your very best, and feel good about it.

"If you do all that you can, and leave the situation to God, then there is no need to feel guilty or to let worry enter your thoughts. Vanadev and I will assist you as much as possible by showing you the methods to follow. But the one who has to produce the effort is you. Every situation you encounter and every emotion you use, including all of the anger you will feel are elements to be accepted and examined. They have all been faced and conquered by me and by Vanadev. Everyone must do it themselves, and it can be done. Remember more than anything, this person you dislike is the Buddha, hidden from view by the blindness of ego, yours and the other person's."

They all went and sat at the river with the water touching their feet as the swell of whiteness and the surge of sound vibrated within them. One with the river, Ishwara's mood and reflections were the same. He sang to this oneness:

"Your singing echoes in me your embrace
nights filled with moonlight and secret meetings
days tossed in sunlight as you ran
through the meadows of jade green
dancing in the light and the shadow.

"Your flute song ripples through the reflected tree
I float ashore in the vibrations of sound.
The dangling leaves hold the song, weakly
soon to release it into the wind.
But you always return to my presence
deep from the depths of your being."

A few weeks later shadows from floating leaves, guided by the mood of the sun, rested impermanently upon the water. With the glance of a ray, the shadows drifted on… A leaf striving to live for all seasons changed color the next day, upon falling, was consumed by the river.

Endless Cycles of Rebirth

Hampered by dryness, red and yellow leaves curl and crack. A leaf drops into shallow water, exposing the sky reflected in it. Transparent and strong, the wind grows, gathering its momentum. The sky runs away and hides, low gray clouds hang, another leaf vibrates, and then falls… There is no defense among the leaves. Vulnerable to each moment, they simply release their hold.

Winds steadily bombard fragile vines, the sockets split and release, to the wind they fly. Distant and obscure, winds once out of reach like a bird on the horizon, approach. Rows of blossoms meander through sage, then to a brook. In the morning there was a flower, at sunset, a stem.

Not far from the river those students who did not have to return to their villages joined Ishwara and Vanadev at a lake. It was silent and still, remnants of feathers rested upon it. Suddenly, a morning rain permeated the water, and as it vibrated, ripples expanded losing their potency as they barely touched the bank and dissipated. The rhythmic balance of the miniature waves continued until evening approached. Then as suddenly as the rains came, they withdrew, and the night was as clear as a crystal water pool.

In the morning, there was a feeling that nature had held all of the summer that it could grasp and it was time to let it go. Within the shelters they built, Ishwara,

Vanadev, and the students watched clouds and shadows reflect in the lake water. A rainbow dominated the sky, and an ever so patient bird held on thoughtlessly to a twig. A wisp of wind brushed it and it darted to a nearby bush. The forest grew crisp in the chilled air.

A withered tree loses its last leaf. Tossed about helplessly to wander in the wind, the leaf is consumed by the river. Rustle-wind-leaves manipulate the silence, piles of leaves begin their journey of decay. Damp air carries the scent of autumn's last breath. The endless pulsation of a fearless winter converges with a season's death. The sky has given over to blotches of gray with black. Day is through, the land roars with rain, night seals the sky in thunder.

When the rain finally finishes the group leaves the bloated lake and begins to walk toward a far mountain. After a day's journey and a few thousand feet higher in elevation, they circle a lake of ice and snow while creatively designed flakes float everywhere. Patterns of silence are woven over the earth, deserted twigs, frozen deer prints, brooks of solid ice. Geese scatter about the snow and fly off, echoing into the distance. Swirling winds enclose them and flurries surround them as enormous white clouds empty their mass. The land is stifled by the whiteness.

Ishwara and Vanadev exhaustedly enter a cave to escape the blizzard. They sit to rest and watch the the snow coming in from the cave opening which flies past their faces and melts on the walls and floor. Beyond the mouth of the cave they see endless acres of white sky empty from the abyss of the heavens. The earth shakes when the sky stampedes. Wind whipped clouds thrash downward smothering the land. Rushing from the petrified lake, drifts of snow merge with the furious mountain air.

Oblivious to the overwhelmed river, thousands of feet below, the dim winter sun panoramically surveys the mountain ranges. A vagrant crane is carried wildly by the updraft. The chilled wind of dawn sweeps across the sky. Covered within the newest veil of lace, the Himalayas pose like an altar smothered in white silk. The ivory mountainsides submit gracefully, forced into hibernation.

After what seems like an eternity, the breath of winter dilutes and the rigidness of winter loosens. Spring opens its arms and embraces the sky and land with warmth. Returning birds turn joyfully in the wind, waves of grass incline toward the sky and deepen with green. Sunlit streams flow with vibration and light, patterned with subtle reflections.

A quiet mountain embraces the breathing of the trees, a distant eagle's nest bears new life. Frogs yawn on lily pads in the early morning. Moss strokes the sides of trees, yellow fungi smother stumps while wild mushrooms sprout. Pine needles and honeysuckle vines scent the air.

Mindfulness

I was led where my form could not follow,
steps without footprints.
Taken to a mountain higher than the air
I plunged into emptiness
while razor-like swords met me in the ravine.

Simultaneously I saw and experienced
unrestricted hatred, cemetery cries, wretched starvation,
grotesque hell beings, burning cold,
intermittent blindness, unimaginable heat,
wretched loneliness, terrifying fear.

I was brought desirable women
and planets of diamonds and gold,
I saw my body in every stage of its death
but I stood firm holding the precious pearl
and the myriad illusions disappeared.

The Master's Light

Cumulative energy revolves through the eyes of continual change of form - the reshaping into emptiness. Like spinning chimes, the seasons pass quickly.

**Somewhere a blossom loosens, falls
another, then another
each reveals its spent individuality
a motion of silence
all soon to be devoured
by the grasping rapids.**

The tune of winter sounds and the circle of seasons come about again. From the gray sky, sun beckons the earth and the land waits for the coming warmth. The frozen roots of plants begin to release their hold on winter.

Golden sun, the object that asks for nothing, spreads its devotion and its promise to the land. An umbrella of warmth spreads, opening lilac scent to the air. Twigs once frozen in ice grow green, the illuminated ground throws the meadow into blush, and wild with color the naked earth takes form. Enlivened by sunlight, winds and colors speed to embrace the emptiness. Grass weaves freely, almost endlessly, and ferns dangle their shades of green over the water.

Flocks of birds whisk through the smooth breeze and bask in the rays, warmed with happiness. Trees spread into the sky and pine-needle-sails dance in the exuberant wind. Warmth stimulates the last hardened branches of winter that grasp anxiously to the breeze blowing by... There is a feeling of expectancy among the groves of oak: a sense of life in rapid motion, buds protrude and decorate the trees. All the drops in all the streams rapidly converge and force their way back to their source, the river. Gathering frozen leaves, sunshine and air, impressions, depth, experience; vibrant in their energy, a million rapids of power rush toward the horizon.

All of the students returned to the river and Ishwara and Vanadev lead a meditation on the earth that concludes with an ancient river mantra. Upon finishing, Vanadev said, "the mantra sounded different, in some cases garbled. The purpose of the river mantra is to become in tune with the river, thus becoming one with the source of its flow. When the breath is not even, the words are not clear, and a person tends to lose concentration. While the Buddha was preaching in Kushinagara, he said that infants extend the stomach when they inhale, but that somewhere along the way in childhood they tend to do the opposite.

"If you were to change your breathing technique back to the original way, you would soon see that it is as natural as your breathing is now. You will have more air to hold the mantra longer, to deepen your voice, and control the stomach muscles so that the amount of air which is released is steady. The stomach muscles will draw in on themselves when the air is used up and the chanting will stop. Therefore what you are focusing on will stay centered in concentration. Your breathing and your being will be more attuned to each other, like the heartbeat when you are walking."

Unequalled Compassion

Prostrations lure my body up and down
the microcosm and the macrocosm,
back and forth, I bow to the Master,
the Buddha, the Dharma, and the Sangha.
Purified with humility, I rise,
the enlightenment thought carried into infinity
as every sound gives birth to the six syllables.

In turn, each being overwhelmed by love
electrifies the air with positive light
issuing from every pore a profusion of Buddhas.
Effortlessly,
Avalokitesvara is placed on crystal moonseat
upon a diamond white lotus, on the head crown
with its roots firmly connected in the chakras
spreading into every nerve in the body.

Spontaneously,
while chanting the most sacred syllables
of the universe itself
Om Mani Padme Hum,
the nectar of Avalokitesvara, sublimely golden
with its honey-like quality, protrudes
through the moonseat and the blossom
down into the head and throughout the body.

**The form is saturated with nectar
purified of all past karma
from wrong inclinations and habitual thinking.
Diseases fade, the body is indestructible.
Immeasurable white light is projected from the heart
touching all beings with compassion and wisdom,
inclusion of oneness.**

**The six realms are perfected
all the world's actions, are our actions
the world's karma, our karma
the world's awakening, our awakening.**

The students asked if he would tell them a story about himself and Shakyamuni. Vanadev said, "after listening to the Buddha tell His life story at Rajagriha the day before, I awoke early and came to sit under a fig tree. Soon the Avatar came and sat next to me. I told him that I could never sit and fast for six years like he did to attain enlightenment. He said that fasting like he had was necessary for the work that He was doing at the time. He said that He had always been enlightened and it was not a level that he had to attain.

"His role as a child-prince and as a husband, father, and teacher was for the benefit of others. He said that sitting for six years was a symbolic example for man's benefit, not His own. He said that He did this because when He preached about enlightenment and the methods to reach it, along with the pitfalls, that for people to understand even a semblance of it, they had to see Him experience it. This was accomplished with a physical-symbolic technique. He added that some children never fully understand or believe their parents until they are actually shown how something works.

"I responded with, 'as I first came to notice You, I was like a dormant seed which needed water to be given a chance at spiritual growth. Upon Your acceptance of my newly chosen path, I became rich with the soil of Your energy and my fears were released. Every lesson that flows from Your wisdom touches me deeply and keeps me in step with the dance of life. Your face is the image of compassion. Help me to extend myself into the 'Oneness' that I seek to return to.'

"He also told me that frozen soil, bombarded by intense sun, eventually thaws into warmth. Young seeds sprout when the perfect conditions are present; the new from the old, the present from the past, a world transformed. Through the stem of inexperience the very first leaves form and take in light. It is a painful process to learn one's own nature. Continually the leaves feel the closeness of the tree and they draw nourishment from the sun, content to be what they are. Just like this, the Buddha said I had matured."

One afternoon Sudrulada and Thrushami went into the middle of the river with Ishwara in the ferryboat. Ishwara asked them what they had learned about sexual energy since their last talk.

Sudrulada replied, "the human form is the perfect channel of consciousness. Matter and energy, the ocean for instance, is not aware of itself. But with mind, our bodies create awareness through the chakras, and the heart guides them to work together. So heart is mind, it is the depth of the mind. The heart is the purifier.

"We are the universe. Our physical, subtle, and mental bodies are matter, energy, and mind. We are of the same energy as the sun. Our chakras allow energy to flow through them from one body to another, and we transmit and receive this energy just as the universe."

Thrushami then added, "a balanced union is one of harmony, where real happiness lies in making your partner happy. Harmony is understanding the oneness of both the male and female parts of your personality. To break down the illusion of "you" as separate from your partner, a person must not be attached to identifying himself or herself with their body. The energy of desire must be transformed and rechanneled into love and appreciation of all the qualities of your lover, and in our marriage we have allowed this process to take place.

"To satisfy all tendencies in expressing love and friendship for your partner through sex, you must transform the energy to a higher form of action. If a person tries to ignore feelings and desires by repressing sexual energy, the energy only becomes more overpowering. To reach the final level in understanding oneness, we must go beyond the physical act of uniting sexual energies and attain total and complete detachment. There cannot be a complete sharing of love until we go beyond expectation and result: not to consume, but to be consumed by love is the essence of real love.

"We thank you a hundred times, Most Accomplished Master, for helping us to understand these things."

"Dear ones," Ishwara replied, "I have shown you the way, but it was both of you who experienced it."

Like The River, Everything Returns

The last rumbling of night clouds dissipates through the sky, revealing the slightest light of sun. The light crawls through a spider's web and the coolness of evening lifts away and melts in the warm air. Mountainside streams drain melted snow and water empties into a pond where it sparkles green then white.

Birds vibrantly sing to the listening wind. Trees still heavy with dew accept the new light. Clear water vibrates and catches the depth and power of the light. The image of peacefulness blends into the Indian earth.

Energized water splashes as a bird dives, embracing the sun and cool water; rippling reflections of a spring awakening sky. Wild reeds grow green and plants flower with buds. Spring grasses straddle the hillsides as the virgin breeze touches them.

Air, pure, cool, and sweet, emits freshness into the embryonic day. All life awakens to the expansive sky that stretches far beyond the vastness of the river. The energy of the water draws symmetry from the earth and the sky, like the oneness of mind and body.

The students asked question after question until night fell. Ishwara had revealed many things to them that night. Among them he said, "the heart was full and complete, the essence of all love, and it was ripe for birth. So the heart opened and the universe was born.

"There was emptiness, and when there was a notion of consciousness there was vapor, wind, liquid, and then solid. From fire, ice, and water, came wind, earth, and sea.

"At the ocean, watch the foam on the sand, see it gather and expand. See the bubbles burst and evaporate like white clouds in a storm. For an eternity, in and out, grow and explode, they play and make patterns in the sand. All in life worth knowing can be understood in just a tiny pocket of air or in a droplet of water, seemingly not even worth noticing. Everything began from everything else, one particle is all particles, all is sameness, and everything is "one"."

Multiplicity

**Round and round the spiraling sound
over and through sail the waves into
the absence of light, fullness of emptiness
the hurricane's spite.
Time, illusion, ceaseless change
imagination gathers the night stars
overwhelmed by the blackness
the new moon sinks into the ocean depths.**

**What one drop knows and feels
ultimately every drop, everywhere
will know and feel,
random shells tumble ashore
foam evaporating in the sand...**

The fresh scented air of a spring morning came rolling over the hills. Echoes of life murmured through the meadow and the constant sun drew up flower stems, one by one taking their first breath. The golden light penetrated and filled them with vital warmth.

Vines sprout into colorful expression. Life blooms into movement and sound, a waterfall glides into a blue lake. Air currents bend into harmonious sway with branches of trees. Butterflies prostrate in the sun's pure presence, then dance ever so delicately. They dip and rise to the continual rhythm in the brook.

From forests lush with fern, dart rainbow hued birds, like wild orchids in the moment of bloom. The birds link the river to the sky as their collage penetrates into the inevitable sunset.

To Buddha's Passing

The flute sings through the bamboo leaves
the dreaminess rises and flows,
movement without form.
Suspended in infinity
the sitar lure pulls the strings in obeisance
for the Voice behind the sound of falling water.

Transformed into nectar light
water is drawn up
to wash the Guru's feet.
Hearts seeking transcendence
heavy with the past of India
search the Bodhi tree for the moment, now.

Buddha's step to each note
plays rhythm with the sun,
a universal walk to non-attachment.
Held gently by the song's breeze
the breath and ashes of the Sacred One
melt into the energy of light.

Ishwara gathered the students by the river to tell them that soon he would be leaving. He said his spiritual work was finished and that Vanadev would continue as their guide.

He said, "within three days I will leave you and the river, and I want to tell you once more about my love for all of you. As the blossom that fills my heart for you expands, so too does the sun spread over the meadow in the morning and evaporate the dew with its light.

"Listen, as the sun speaks without sound. Hear the soundlessness as the light breeds forth a sprout. The land is alive and filled with energy, as is our positive connection with each other. Now is the time for spiritual maturity, when my thoughts and energy are immersed in your light: the time when the sun cannot burn bright enough to nurture my feelings toward you all, which only your closeness can ripen.

"It is the time when you and I, like the sky and the sun, remain one and never part, the time to complete each other and have no mysteries; the blossoming of two flowers, two identities, two universes, becoming 'one'."

Embraces followed tears and feelings of appreciation, and of course regret. Confusion filled the minds of those who thought they could not go on without the one they so dearly loved. But Ishwara told them that Vanadev was his successor, and that their devotion toward him should be given unconditionally to Vanadev.

They responded by saying that they know and love Vanadev, and of course would always follow his instruction, but their sorrow stemmed from the thought of not seeing him again, and they were not ready to separate from him. Just then they realized what Ishwara meant when he told them about oneness. Their feelings were sincere, but they knew there was no such thing as separation. Whatever respect and devotion they had toward Ishwara, they would also find the same transmission energy in Vanadev.

In three days Ishwara stood on the bank of the river, ready to return to it. With all the disciples surrounding him, Vanadev said to Ishwara, "great teacher and ancient friend, the source of my heart, I reveal that I love you in all that is within me to know. We are the fire and the flame, one within each other. I most humbly offer you my heart."

One last embrace from everyone led Ishwara into the ferryboat, and as he stood facing the endless river he spoke to it, "I have heard you singing on a thousand warm nights in the blissful breeze, I have watched you swirl with rhythms and vibrations, dark and still and reflecting. My voice will not allow me to speak of the ways which one can love you, only my heart can reveal such beauty.

"Remain ever-moving and yet motionless, while you absorb the energy of the sun. I will remain silent in anticipation of this admiration as I flow into your consciousness, my universal reflection."

Ishwara turned and bowed low to Vanadev, then to the disciples. As he pushed the pole into the mud, he smiled. His eyes were held on them until he was far down the river. As quickly as it takes the water to flow from cove to cove, he was gone, *no time, no distance, no sorrow...*